VALERIE THOMAS AND KORKY PAUL

Winnie AND Wilbur
GADGETS GALORE

Winnie AND Wilbur IN SPACE

Winnie AND Wilbur: THE NEW COMPUTER

Winnie AND Wilbur: THE BIG BAD ROBOT

OXFORD
UNIVERSITY PRESS

Winnie AND Wilbur
IN SPACE

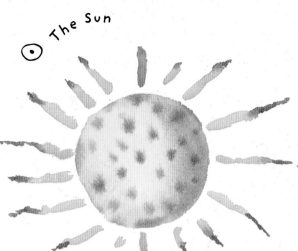

The Sun

Winnie the Witch loved to look through her telescope at the night sky.

It was huge and dark and mysterious. 'I'd love to go into space, Wilbur,' Winnie would say. 'It would be such a big adventure.'

Wilbur, Winnie's big black cat, loved to be outside at night too. He liked to chase moths and bats and shadows.

That was enough adventure for Wilbur.

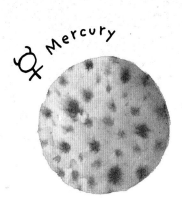

☿ Mercury

Then one night, when the Moon and stars were bright, Winnie suddenly said, 'Let's go into space right now, Wilbur!'

'Meeow?' said Wilbur.

'But how will we get there?' wondered Winnie. 'We need a rocket, and I don't have a rocket.' Then she looked up at the Moon, and she had a wonderful idea.

She waved her magic wand, shouted,

'Abracadabra!'

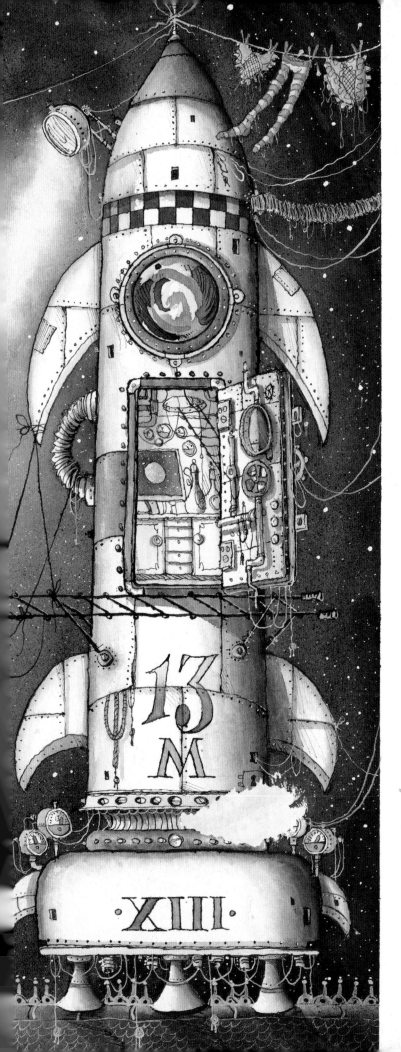

Venus

. . . and there, on the roof, was a rocket. Winnie packed a picnic basket, got her Big Book of Spells, just in case, and ran up the stairs with Wilbur.

Winnie shut her eyes, waved her magic wand, and shouted,

'Abracadabra!'

10
9
8
7
6
5
4 . . .

Earth

3
2
1 . . . .

The rocket shot off
the roof and into space.
It went very, very fast.
And it was hard to steer.

'Oops!'
Winnie nearly flew
into a satellite.

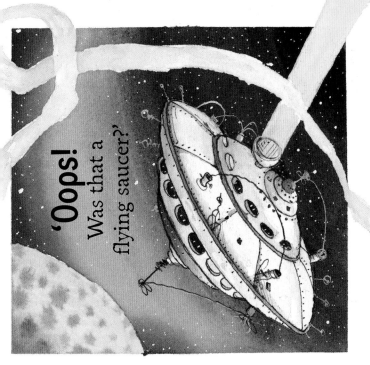

'Oops! Was that a flying saucer?'

'Oops! That was a falling star, Wilbur!'

WHOOSH!

The Moon

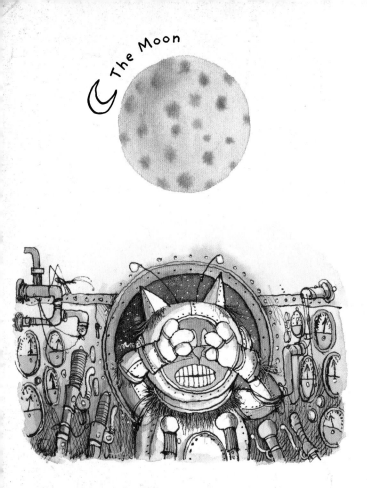

'**Meeow!**' said Wilbur.
He put his paws over his eyes.

'We'll find a lovely planet for our
picnic, Wilbur,' Winnie said.

Wilbur peeped out from
behind his paws. There were
little planets everywhere.

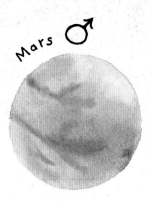

Mars ♂

'Here's a sweet little planet,' Winnie said. 'We'll have our picnic here.'

'**Purr!**' said Wilbur. He loved picnics.

PLOP! The rocket landed. All was quiet and peaceful. But there were funny little holes everywhere. Wilbur looked down the holes. They seemed to be empty . . .

Winnie unpacked the food. There were pumpkin scones, chocolate muffins, some cherries, and cream for Wilbur. **Yum!**

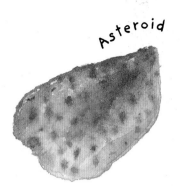
Asteroid

A little head popped out of a hole, and then there were heads everywhere.

'Rabbits!' said Winnie. 'Space rabbits are coming to our picnic!'

'Meeow!' said Wilbur.

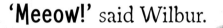

A space rabbit hopped over to try some cream.
Yuck!

Another space rabbit tried a pumpkin scone.
Horrible.

Chocolate muffins?
Disgusting.
Cherries?
Yuck!

Then some of the space rabbits
hopped over to the rocket.

They sniffed it . . .

♃ Jupiter

and took a bite. Then the rocket was covered in space rabbits.

'Oh no!' shouted Winnie. She waved her magic wand, shouted, 'Abracadabra!'

and carrots and lettuces rained down on the rabbits. But the space rabbits didn't like carrots or lettuces.

'Of course!' said Winnie. She waved her magic wand, shouted, 'Abracadabra!'

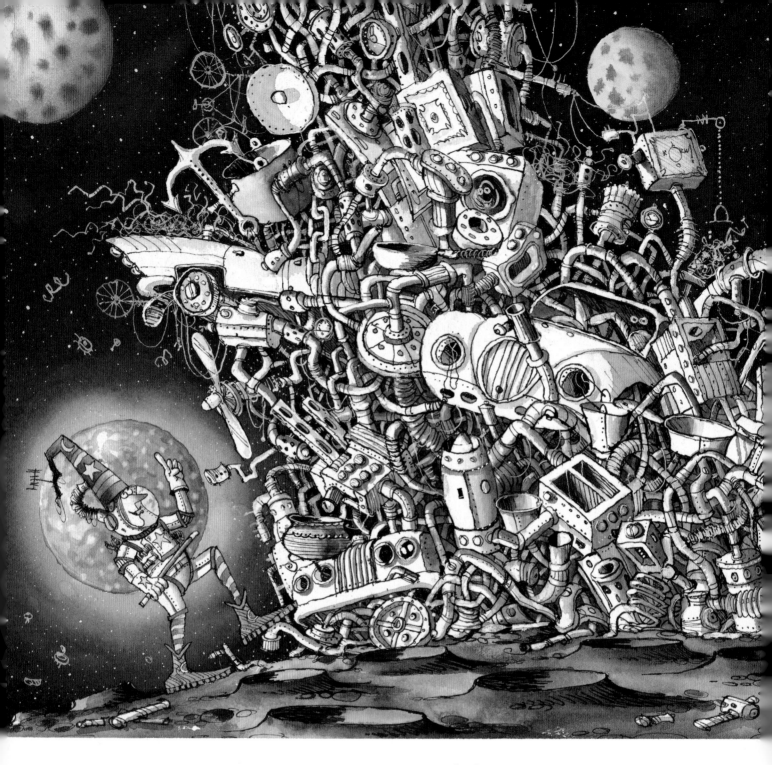

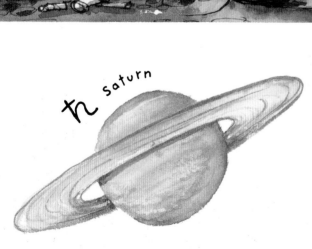
ℏ saturn

. . . and there was a giant
pile of metal.

Saucepans,
wheelbarrows,
bicycles,
cars,
even a fire engine.

Yes! That was what space rabbits liked.

Scrumptious!
But it was too late . . .

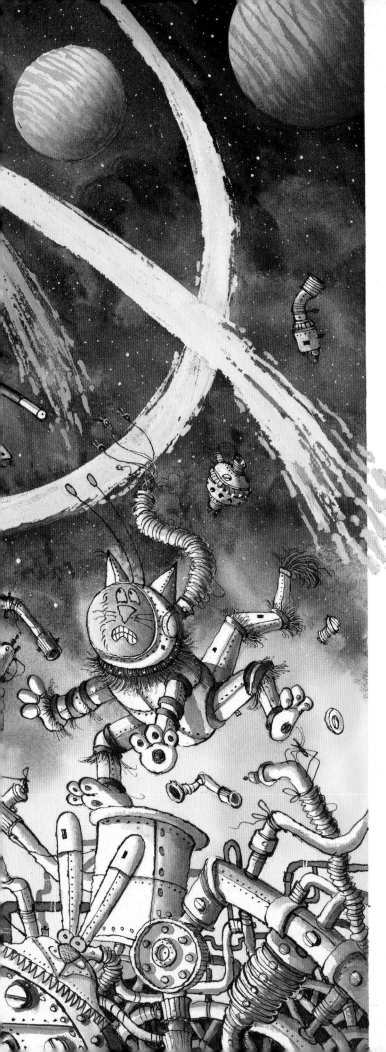

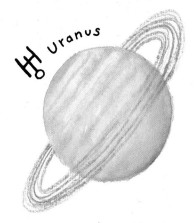

Uranus

the space rabbits had eaten up all of Winnie's metal rocket.

'Blithering broomsticks!' shouted Winnie. 'Now how will we get home?'

'**Meeeow!**' said Wilbur.

Winnie looked at the giant pile of metal. 'Perhaps,' she said. 'Maybe. I wonder.'

She looked in her Big Book of Spells. 'Yes!' she said.

Then she picked up her magic wand, waved it five times, and shouted,

'Abracadabra!'

There was a flash of fire, a bang . . .

Neptune

and there, on top of the giant pile of metal, was a rattling, roaring scrap metal rocket.

Winnie and Wilbur climbed up to the rattling, roaring rocket and jumped in.

vrOOM!

The rocket blasted away.
It rushed and roared
through space.

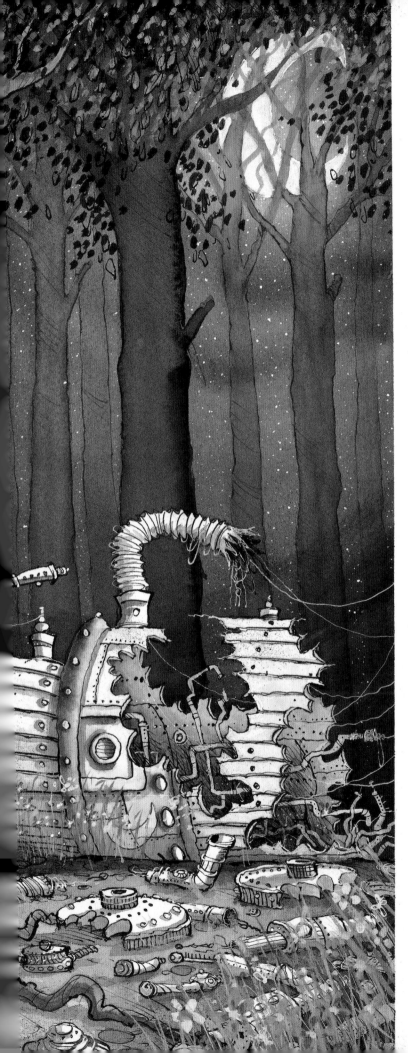

Pluto

WHUMP!

The rocket landed in Winnie's garden.

'That was an adventure, Wilbur,' Winnie said. 'But I'm glad we're home.'

'**P**urr, purr, purr,' said Wilbur.

He was very glad to be home.

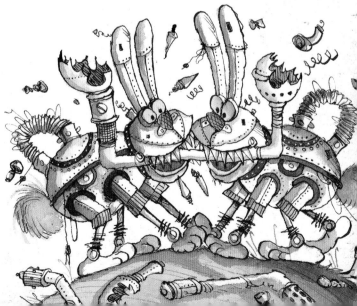

Winnie and Wilbur

THE NEW COMPUTER

Winnie the Witch had a new
computer. She was very excited.
Her cat, Wilbur, was excited too.
He thought something interesting
might happen and he didn't
want to miss it.

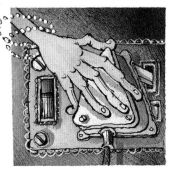

Winnie plugged in the computer,
turned it on, and clicked the mouse.
'Come on, mouse,' she said.

Is that a *mouse*? thought Wilbur.
It doesn't look like one.

CLICK CLICK

Winnie went on to the internet.
Wilbur wanted a closer look at the mouse.
He patted it.

'Don't touch the mouse, Wilbur!' said Winnie.
'I want to order a new wand!'

Wilbur patted the mouse again. **Pat, pat.**

Winnie was cross.
She put Wilbur outside.
She didn't notice
that it was raining . . .

Wilbur noticed it was raining. He was getting
wet. He watched Winnie through the window.
She was having a good time.

She ordered her new wand, and then
she visited some websites for witches.
They had some very funny jokes.
'Ha, ha, ha,' laughed Winnie.

Wilbur *wasn't* laughing.
The rain was dripping off his whiskers.
'Meeow,' he cried. 'Meeeoooww!'
But Winnie didn't hear him.

plop plop plop plop plop
plop plop plop plop plop plop Plop

Plop, plop, plop.
'What's that noise?'
asked Winnie.

It was the rain.
It was coming through the roof.

'Oh no!' said Winnie. 'The rain
will ruin my new computer!
I need the Roof Repair Spell.'

But she couldn't find her Book of Spells
or her magic wand anywhere.

'Oh, where are they?' she cried
as the rain plopped down.

At last she found them.
She waved her wand seven
times at the roof, and shouted,

'Abracadabra!'

The roof stopped leaking.
'Thank goodness,' Winnie said.

Then she had a wonderful idea.

'If I scan all my spells into the computer,' she said,
'I won't need my Book of Spells any more.
I won't need to wave my magic wand.
I'll just use the computer. One click will do the trick.'

So Winnie loaded all her spells into the new computer.
'I'd better try it out,' she said. 'What shall I do?'

'I know, I'll turn Wilbur into a blue cat.'

She let Wilbur inside. She went to
the computer, clicked the mouse,
and Wilbur was bright blue.

'Good!' said Winnie.
'It works!'

CLICK

CLICK

She clicked the mouse, and Wilbur was a black cat again.
An angry, wet, black cat.

'Well, Wilbur,' said Winnie, 'I won't need my
Book of Spells or my magic wand any more.'

And she put them out for the
dustman to take away.

That night, Wilbur waited until
he could hear Winnie snoring.
Then he crept downstairs.

He was going to see about that mouse.

He patted it.
Nothing happened.
'Meeow, grrrrsssss!' he snarled.
He grabbed the mouse, tossed it
into the air, and rolled onto his back.

Winnie had a lovely sleep.
In the morning she came downstairs
for her breakfast.

'Breakfast, Wilbur,' she called.
'Where are you, Wilbur?'

She looked in the garden, in the bathroom, in all the cupboards.
No Wilbur. Then she looked in the computer room . . .

'OH NO!!!' cried Winnie.
'Wilbur, where are you? And where's the computer?'

She reached into the cupboard for her Book of Spells. She put her hand in her pocket for her magic wand.

Then she remembered.

She ran to the window. The dustman was tipping her rubbish into his truck.

'Stop!' shouted Winnie. 'STOP!' But it was too late. The dustman couldn't hear her. He jumped into his truck and drove away.

'What shall I do?' cried Winnie.

Then another truck came through the gate.
'My new wand!' said Winnie.
'It's arrived! Thank goodness!'

She grabbed the new wand, waved it once, and shouted,

'Abracadabra!'

The Book of Spells flew out of the
rubbish truck, up into the air . . .

. . . and dropped into her arms.

Winnie rushed inside, and looked up the spell to make things come back.
Then she shut her eyes, waved her wand four times, and shouted,

'Abracadabra!'

The computer and Wilbur came back.
'Oh, Wilbur!' said Winnie. 'You're bright blue!
Whatever happened?
Never mind, I'll change you back to black again.'

She went to the computer
and clicked the mouse.
Wilbur was a black cat again.

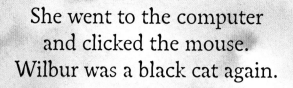

'Good,' said Winnie.
'It still works. But I think I'll keep my
Book of Spells and my magic wand.
I might need them one day.'

Winnie AND Wilbur
THE BIG BAD ROBOT

Every Wednesday afternoon Winnie the Witch and her big black cat Wilbur went to art classes in the library.

They learned how to paint
and draw, knit and sew,
make pots and posters,
and lots of other things.
Winnie the Witch really
enjoyed *all* of the classes.

Wilbur enjoyed *some* of them.

This Wednesday they were making models.
Winnie decided to make a bear.

She chose a cardboard box for the head.

She glued on the eyes, nose, and mouth.

Then she made the body,

arms,

and legs.

It looked good. The teacher liked it too.

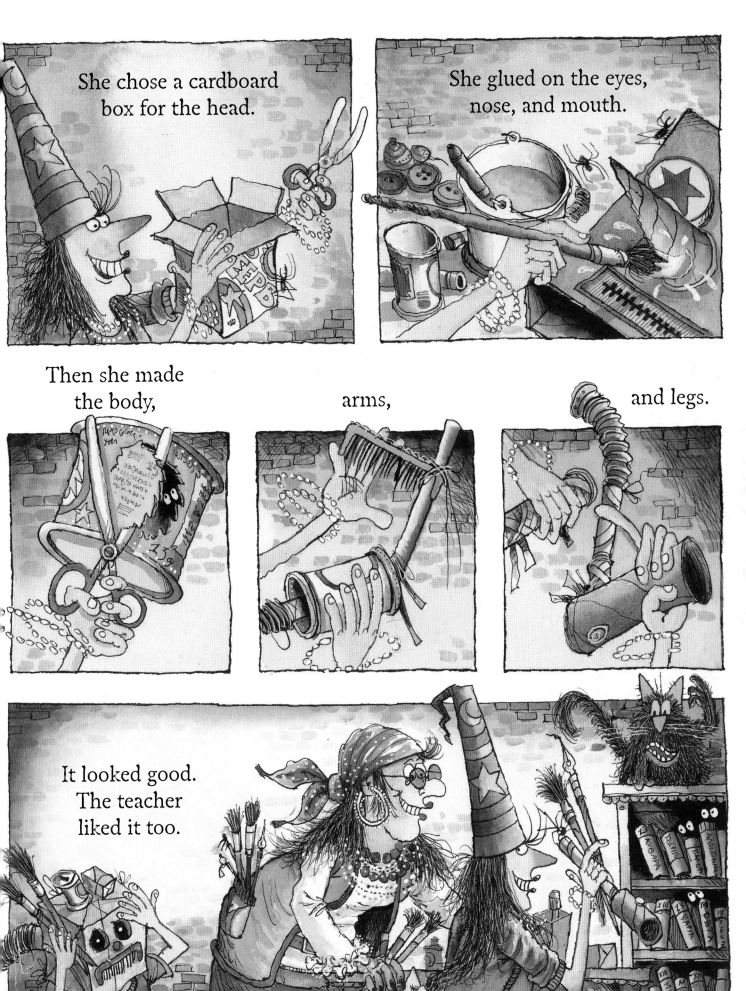

'That's a lovely robot you've made, Winnie,' she said. Winnie was cross. *A robot?*

But when she looked at it carefully, it did look a bit like a robot. Everybody admired it.

Winnie sat the robot on her broomstick.
Then Winnie, Wilbur, and the robot flew home.

Winnie stood the robot on the kitchen table.
'It's a pity it's not a real robot,' she said.

Then Winnie had an idea.
She picked up her magic
wand, shouted,

'Abracadabra!'

. . . and there in the kitchen was a real robot.
'Beep, beep, beep,' said the robot.
Its eyes flashed red and green.

Winnie was delighted.
'Isn't this a lovely robot, Wilbur?' Winnie said.

Wilbur didn't think so.
The robot walked over to
Wilbur and pulled his tail.
'Yeeoww!' cried Wilbur.

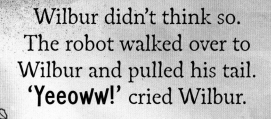

'Naughty robot!' Winnie said.
'You mustn't pull poor Wilbur's tail!'

The robot looked at Winnie.
Then it leaned over and pinched her nose.
'Oww!' said Winnie. 'That hurt.
I've made a bad robot, Wilbur.
I'll change it back into a model.'

Winnie went to pick up her magic wand.
But the robot was too fast for her.

It grabbed
Winnie's wand,

walked up the wall,

across the ceiling,

and then out of the window.

'Oh no!' shouted Winnie.
'My wand still has the robot spell on it, Wilbur.
We have to get it back.'

Winnie and Wilbur tiptoed
out of the front door.
They hid behind the tallest tree.

The big bad robot
was waving Winnie's wand.

Two robot frogs jumped into the pond.
Three robot ducks flew across the sky.
The robot waved the wand again and
four robot rabbits hopped across the grass.

Then the robot waved the wand
at Winnie's front door . . .

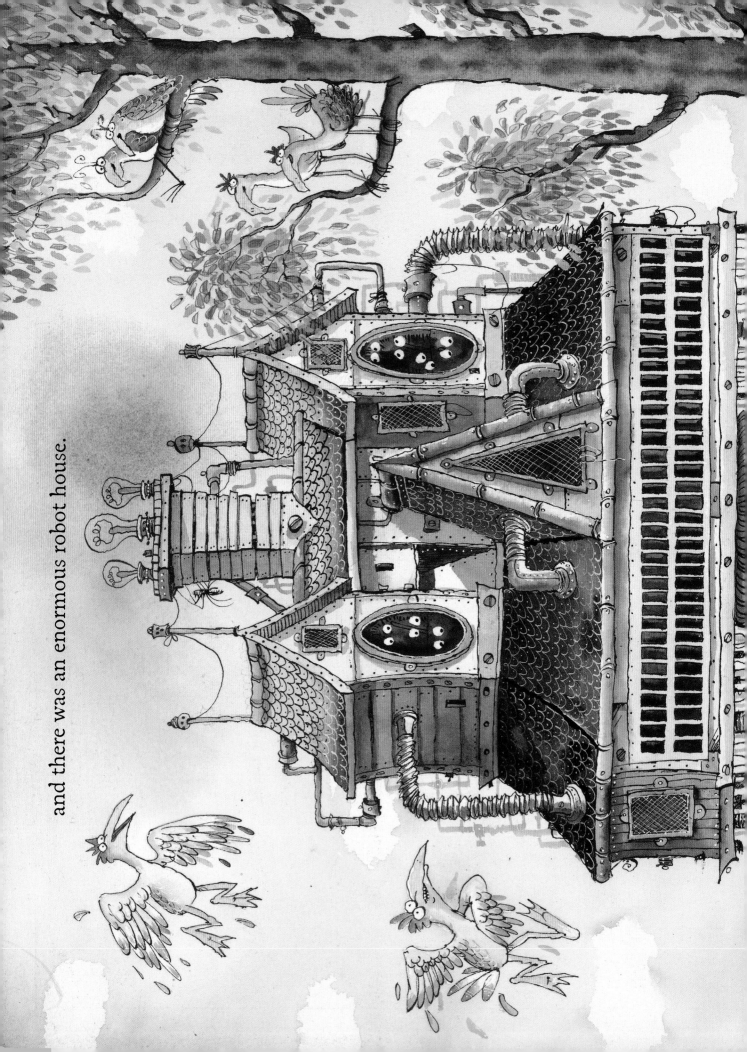

and there was an enormous robot house.

Winnie waited
until the robot
walked past the tree.

She jumped out,

'Blithering
broomsticks!'
Winnie whispered.
'My lovely house is
a robot house!
We have to get my
wand back, Wilbur.'

and Winnie the Witch was Winnie the Robot.

Oh no!

Winnie the Robot walked round and round
the garden.
'**Beep, beep, beep,**' she said.

'**Meeoow!**' said Wilbur.
He didn't like Winnie the Robot.
He wanted Winnie the Witch back again.
He would have to get Winnie's wand.

But how?

Wilbur had an excellent idea.

He grabbed a creeper . . .

swung out over the big
bad robot, and snatched
Winnie's wand.

Then he swung across to Winnie the Robot,

and
dropped
the
wand
into
her
hand.

Winnie the Robot waved the wand
again and again, and shouted,

'Abra-beep-beep-cadabra...'

Two frogs jumped into the pond,
three ducks flew up into the sky,
four rabbits hopped across the grass,
the robot house was Winnie's house,
Winnie the Robot was Winnie the Witch,
and instead of a big bad robot there was
a little pile of junk.

Winnie the Witch flopped down
into her deckchair.
Wilbur curled up in her lap.

'Thank you, Wilbur,' Winnie said.
'I am very lucky to have such a clever cat.'
'Purr, purr, purr,' said Wilbur.

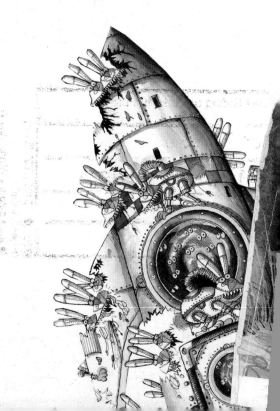

OXFORD
UNIVERSITY PRESS

Great Clarendon Street, Oxford OX2 6DP

Oxford University Press is a department of the University
of Oxford. It furthers the University's objective of excellence
in research, scholarship, and education by publishing worldwide.
Oxford is a registered trade mark of Oxford University Press in
the UK and in certain other countries

Database right Oxford University Press (maker)

Winnie and Wilbur: The New Computer first published as *Winnie's New Computer* in 2003
Winnie and Wilbur in Space first published as *Winnie in Space* in 2010
Winnie and Wilbur: The Big Bad Robot first published as *Winnie's Big Bad Robot* in 2014
Winnie and Wilbur: Gadgets Galore first published in 2017

The stories are complete and unabridged

British Library Cataloguing in Publication Data available

ISBN: 978-0-19-275849-1

10 9 8 7 6 5 4 3 2 1

Printed in China

Paper used in the production of this book is a natural, recyclable
product made from wood grown in sustainable forests. The
manufacturing process conforms to the environmental
regulations of the country of origin

www.winnieandwilbur.com